The Wolf's Chicken Stew

Keiko Kasza

G. P. Putnam's Sons   New York

Copyright © 1987 by Keiko Kasza

All rights reserved. This book, or parts thereof,
may not be reproduced in any form without permission
in writing from the publishers.
Published simultaneously in Canada.
Printed in Hong Kong by South China Printing Co.
Designed by Martha Rago

Library of Congress Cataloging in Publication Data
Kasza, Keiko.   The wolf's chicken stew.
Summary: A hungry wolf's attempts to fatten a
chicken for his stewpot have unexpected results.
[1. Wolves—Fiction. 2. Chickens—Fiction] 1. Title
PZ7.K15645Wo 1987   [E]   86-12303
ISBN 0-399-22000-3 (Sandcastle pbk)
1   3   5   7   9   10   8   6   4   2
ISBN 0-399-21400-3 (hc)
5   7   9   10   8   6

To Gregory

There once lived a wolf who loved to eat more than anything else in the world. As soon as he finished one meal, he began to think of the next.

One day the wolf got a terrible craving for chicken stew.

All day long he walked across the forest in search of a delicious chicken. Finally he spotted one.

"Ah, she is just perfect for my stew," he thought.

The wolf crept closer. But just as he was about to grab his prey …

he had another idea.

"If there were just some way to
fatten this bird a little more," he
thought, "there would be all the
more stew for me." So ...

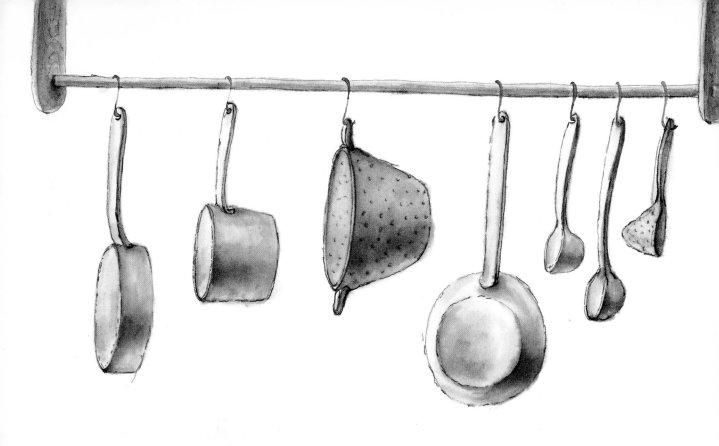

the wolf ran home to his kitchen,
and he began to cook.

First he made a hundred scrumptious
pancakes. Then, late at night,
he left them on the chicken's porch.

   "Eat well, my pretty chicken,"
he cried. "Get nice and fat for my
stew!"

The next night he brought a
hundred scrumptious doughnuts.
   "Eat well, my pretty chicken,"
he cried. "Get nice and fat for my
stew!"

And on the next night he brought
a scrumptious cake weighing a
hundred pounds.

"Eat well, my pretty chicken,"
he cried. "Get nice and fat for my
stew!"

At last, all was ready. This was the
night he had been waiting for. He
put a large stew pot on the fire
and set out joyfully to find his
dinner.

"That chicken must be as fat as a
balloon by now," he thought.
"Let's see."

But as he peeked into the
chicken's house …

the door opened suddenly and the chicken
screeched, "Oh, so it was you, Mr. Wolf!"

"Children, children! Look, the
pancakes and the doughnuts
and that scrumptious cake —
they weren't from Santa Claus!
All those presents were from
Uncle Wolf!"

The baby chicks jumped all over
the wolf and gave him a hundred
kisses.

"Oh, thank you, Uncle Wolf!
You're the best cook in the world!"

Uncle Wolf didn't have chicken
stew that night but Mrs. Chicken
fixed him a nice dinner anyway.

"Aw, shucks," he thought, as
he walked home, "maybe tomor-
row I'll bake the little critters a
hundred scrumptious cookies!"

Date Due

FEB 25 '92	APR 28 '94	MAR 19 '95	FEB 13 '03
MAY 7 '92	SEP 20 '94	Dec 10 '96	FEB 27 '03
OCT 22 '92	JAN 13 '95	1-14-97	APR 17 '03
NOV 11 '92	SEP 26 '95	OCT 30 '97	OCT 08 '03
NOV 19 '92	NOV 14 '95	NOV 10 '97	JAN 13 '04
APR 1 '95	NOV 17 '95	FEB 9 '98	JAN 20 '04
APR 20 '93	DEC 19 '95	11/25/98	JAN 27 '04
APR 27 '95	JAN 2 '96	12-2-98	
MAY 4 '93	Jan 30	1-29	FEB 10 '04
MAY 11 '93	APR 29 '97	2-19	FEB 17 '04
MAY 27 '93	MAY 13 '96	APR 23 '01	FEB 24 '04
OCT 20 '93	OCT 2 '97	MAY 1 '01	MAR 02 '04
NOV 3 '95	1-1-25	MAY 22 '01	MAR 16 '04
DEC 1 '93		MAY 29 '01 OCT 18 '01	MAR 16 '04
APR 13 '94			MAR 31 '04
APR 19 '94		NOV 07 '01	APR 06 '04